1/14

THUMPY
The Christms Hound

by:

Douglas Worth

tate publishing
CHILDREN'S DIVISION

D1417761

Published by Tate Publishing & Enterprises, LLC
127 E. Trade Center Terrace | Mustang, Oklahoma 73064 USA
1.888.361.9473 | www.tatepublishing.com

Tate Publishing is committed to excellence in the publishing industry. The company reflects the philosophy established by the founders, based on Psalm 68:11,
"The Lord gave the word and great was the company of those who published it."

Book design copyright © 2013 by Tate Publishing, LLC. All rights reserved.
Cover design by Joseph Emnace
Interior design by Gram Telen
Illustrations by Dindo Contento

Published in the United States of America

ISBN: 978-1-62902-864-4
1. Juvenile Fiction / Animals / Dogs
2. Juvenile Fiction / Holidays & Celebrations / Christmas & Advent
13.10.21

Dedication

For Col and Dan

All settled and snug? No more orders for juice?
Doors to be shut? Untucked sheets on the loose?

Cats stealing pillows? Alarm clocks unwound?
Missions to check out some dim shape or sound?

Trips to the bathroom with rest stops to see
Through the railing one glittering edge of the tree?

Peeks out the window to learn if that patter
Is just freezing rain or the snow-muffled clatter

Of miniature hooves? "Come on, Daddy, you know
We're ready and waiting. A story! Let's go!"

Okay. You remember how, last Christmas Eve,
I told you a tale somewhat hard to believe,

Unless you rely on your heart, not your mind—
A method toward which, I admit, I'm inclined.

I could tell it again, though perhaps you'd prefer
Another where new Christmas wonders occur…

"Tell a new one!" All right—I'll see what I can do,
But there's no guarantee when you try something new.

Well now, let's see… It could be about mice
In the stockings or bats in the tree might be nice…

The ox in the stable? A marzipan frog!
Or— "No. Tell us one where the hero's a dog."

A dog? Hmmm, a dog. A dog's good, though I'd say
A trifle, well, common…but have it your way.

Now what should our hero be called? Whiskers? Wag?
Not Fido or Rover! Tickbiter? Fleabag?

We could rhyme it with Grumpy…not Slumpy—wrong sound!
Maybe Stumpy? No…Thumpy! The old Christmas hound!

"Why Thumpy?" Well, he was just that sort of creature—
A hard-bitten scratcher, an expert flea reacher

Who thumped through his morning and afternoon naps
Or when sulking, after a few kicks or slaps,

For Thumpy, I'm terribly sorry to say
Was badly mistreated, an unwanted stray

Who scrounged for his supper each evening—but wait,
Let me start at the start so I'll get his tale straight,

So to speak. Long ago, before airplanes and cars,
Before uncles at Christmas with drinks and cigars,

Before Christmas itself was a word so well worn,
For Jesus was just getting set to be born,

In a faraway land, in a town, at an inn
That had seen better days, lived a young dog, so thin

You could see his— "But, Daddy, you said he was old."
I did? Are you sure? When? "Just now, when you told

How his name should be Thumpy, the *old* Christmas hound."
Oh yes, I remember. It seems that you've found

A small contradiction. Well, let's call him neither,
(Although, for that matter, he could have been either.)

Let's say middle-aged—like your mommy and me
(Don't tell her I said so!)—around forty-three,

In dog years, that is—a respectable age
When squirrels and cats are no longer the rage

But bones are the in thing to dig up and gnaw
While scratching an ear with a lazy hind paw,

Except Thumpy rarely had something to dig—
He was, as I say, the reverse of a pig:

Bone skinny, his ribs like a washboard showed through
His coat, which, a good size too large—maybe two—

Nearly slid off his shoulders; his tail was a rat's
His dewlaps so loose he was laughed at by cats!

Altogether, he was a most sad-looking stray
Who barely survived on the scraps thrown away

By the inn, which were often no more than a crust
Of greasy bread tossed in a pail cracked with rust,

Plus what he could turn up on his nightly tour
Of trash cans set out by the neighboring poor.

But one thing distinguished this dog of small note:
The eyes that looked out from his tick-ridden coat

Were the eyes of a dreamer. Don't laugh now—it's true:
Two deep-gazing orbs of a dream-cloudy blue,

Which came from his great-grandsire's mother, I'm told,
Who was a great hunter and won cups of gold

For her beloved master, the king. How a cur
In such sad shape as Thumpy descended from her

I can't say—most likely some passing affair
With a stranger who wooed from a back palace stair—

I really don't know—but I do know his eyes
Seemed to go on forever, like oceans or skies,

And that somewhere, smoldering, deep in the veins
Of our hero, some embers, the buried remains

Of his ancestor's courage, devotion, and pride,
Lay waiting to flame out from his mangy hide.

But no one sensed any such glimmering sparks
In the mongrel whose long days were dimmed by remarks

Like "Bad dog!" and "Git! You old flea-bitten hound!"
Till Thumpy would drag himself over the ground

Toward the stable out back where he'd slink off to sleep
In a manger surrounded by cattle and sheep,

Undisturbed there, except by the taunts of those cats
And the scrabblings and squeals of a gang of huge rats

Who liked to leap up on the trough's edge and gnaw
Until the dog woke, raised his head from a paw,

And growled; then they'd snicker, their dark eyes agleam,
While Thumpy sank back to his favorite dream

In which he'd been dining on pies stuffed with mince
As he sat at the feet of a gentle young prince

Whom he'd rescued from wolves one day out in a blizzard—
That night he had rump steak and fillets of gizzard!

Now once, to pick up the loose thread of my story,
When Caesar Augustus was basking in glory

And colorful proud Roman banners unfurled
In cities and towns throughout most of the world

And at every frontier a fierce Roman legion
Was poking spears into some unconquered region,

Word went out from Rome that the world should be taxed,
(I suppose Caesar felt he had been too relaxed

In putting the squeeze on the people of Rome
And wanted more spears or a new palace dome).

So millions and millions of folks on that morn,
Were ordered to go back to where they were born

To pay and be checked off: sick, lame, blind, or old
Or nursing young babies, through storm, drought, or cold

They had to get going, for back then, I guess
They didn't have such things as postal express

For sending your great-aunt fresh flowers or honey
Or helping the government to collect money

For building more weapons they say will keep peace
(Though to me that's like dressing up lions in fleece

And sending them in to look after the sheep!)
Plus a few extra coins for the leaders to keep

So they can vacation in some sunny spot
Where the poor and such troubling distractions are not.

So everyone, grumbling and mumbling, "Unfair!"
Set out for their hometowns with nothing to wear

But what they could tote as they walked, rode, or jogged—
The hotels were jammed up, the inns were all clogged,

Families camping by roadsides, beneath trees, in fields,
Till urged on by soldiers with bright spears and shields.

In one little corner of this worldwide throng
Joseph and Mary were plodding along

Toward Bethlehem—Mary, as everyone knows,
So pregnant she couldn't look down at her toes

Which is hardly the time for a woman to travel
On donkey-back, over roads strewn with loose gravel,

But Caesar had spoken, and what Caesar said
Could make an old dying man hop out of bed!

So on they went slowly, and stopping to rest
Every hour or so, Mary doing her best

Not to complain, Joseph raging at Rome,
Half-tempted to just turn around and go home;

Until toward one evening, they came to the town
And paused by an inn. Brushing dust from her gown,

Mary quite suddenly clutched at her womb,
Cried out, and said, "Joseph, go ask for a room—

It's time! Joseph rushed in and did all he could,
But whether because of his coarse, dusty hood

Or the fact that they really were filled up that night,
The innkeeper, scowling, a man sour with spite,

Barked out, "No rooms!" and was turning away,
Then turned back. "Unless you'd be willing to stay

"In our stable out back, I could give you half price
If you wouldn't mind sharing with cattle and mice."

Joseph glared at the greedy man scratching his loins
And growled out, "We'll take it!" and put down his coins.

And so they went into the stable that night,
And Joseph made beds of piled straw and a bite

Of supper, which poor Mary had to refuse,
For soon, there, surrounded by donkeys and ewes,

(No doctors or nurses, just Joseph close by)
She gave birth with scarcely a murmur or cry,

To Jesus, who many believe was God's son,
Though others say no, but at least, he was one

Who grew up to be a remarkable man
And proved by example that all of us can

Live much more simply, with less strife and greed
And help one another to get what we need,

Which is why we give presents to honor his birth—
And if everybody all over the earth,

Would take less and give more, who knows? Wars might cease
And the whole world at last live in friendship and peace—

But that's a far matter of someday and maybe…
Getting back to my story, that night, still a baby,

Jesus lay wrapped in a manger that Mary
Had lined with hay, too young to know it was scary

To be lying in moonlight, his mommy asleep,
Amid coughings and shufflings of oxen and sheep,

Half-remembering voices and more than one head
That glimmered with gold as it bowed to his bed,

Looking up to dim rafters now, and the surprise
In a pair of blue, down-gazing, dream-cloudy eyes.

"My prince!" was the phrase that popped into the head
Of our hero as he peered down into that bed.

He'd spent the whole evening making his rounds,
Sniffing and poking through stale coffee grounds

And melon rinds, claiming that night for his own,
Three moldy potato skins and a soup bone.

Then returned to the inn with his belly still growling,
And got quite a shock as he came slowly prowling

Around to the stable—for there was a crowd
Of shepherds, and over their voices the loud

Cries of the innkeeper, rushing about
Waving his fat arms and shrieking, "Get out!"

Until, in a fast-spreading hush, there appeared
Three men upon camels, each with a long beard,

(The men, of course!) wearing rich robes and a crown,
Who spoke to the frantic man till he calmed down

And making a bow, went off stroking his chin
While the men got down, unpacked some things, and went in.

Poor Thumpy, astonished by all these events,
Retreated and lay taking in the strange scents

From under the inn's back steps, while he explored
A fresh batch of fleas that had just hopped aboard,

In an hour or so, when the shepherds had gone,
The three kings, who Thumpy had feared would stay on,

Came out and remounted, each turning his beast,
And trotted off slowly somewhere, heading east.

Thumpy waited another half hour then came out,
Approaching with caution and sniffing about.

He could tell that there still were some people inside
And he thought, for a moment, that he'd better hide

Somewhere else for the night—but some sense drew him on.
At the doorway he stopped, gave a quick nervous yawn,

And poked his head in. Near the spot where he slept
Lay a man and a woman, asleep. As he crept

Farther in, he heard strange cooing sounds from the trough
That served for his bed, and he nearly ran off,

But advanced, step by step, till he came to the manger,
Looked in, and beheld there a softly wrapped stranger.

He should have been frightened—he knew in his mind
That people gave curses and kicks to his kind—

But somehow that small, helpless baby could send
No fear through the dog—he seemed more like a friend

To be watched over, and all the hurts he'd received
Faded away, and at once he believed

That here was the prince of his dreams, come at last,
To brighten his days and make up for the past.

His floppy ears raised, and his brows gave a twitch,
And he even resisted a bothersome itch

And wagging his tail, stood there, resting his head
On the edge of the trough, softly whining instead.

He stood, looking down, for ten minutes or so
Basking in happiness and the soft glow

That came from bright starlight and moonlight outside
Shining down on the baby, his eyes open wide.

He might have stood longer, he would have stood years
Without making a scratch or a flop of his ears

If he'd been allowed to, lost in the supreme
Rapture of standing guard over his dream,

But suddenly something, a scuffling, broke through
His reverie, and without turning, he knew

What was making the sound—it was one of that pack
of large vicious rats scrabbling round for a snack.

Thumpy stiffened! A low growl took shape in his throat
And came welling up in gruff snarls at each note

Of those paws coming closer—and then he saw rise
At one end of the manger, the black beady eyes

Of the battle-scarred leader. It gnawed at the wood
While staring at Thumpy, then leapt up and stood

Twitching its whiskers and licking its lips
As it took in the scent of the child in small sips.

A howl burst from Thumpy—a deep, baying sound
That his great-great-grandmother, Beersheba Hound,

Would have been proud of—the rat slid away
And scurried off somewhere at that mighty bay.

But Joseph, in terror, leapt up from the ground
And saw at the manger the shape of a hound

Its fangs bared and gleaming! He shouted and reached
For his staff and came charging, while poor Mary screeched.

Our hero, his dream shattered, cowered and fled
Out of the stable from his prince's bed

Back under the steps, while the man stopped and stood
Glaring out into darkness, and then, as he could

Blocked the door shut with old crates—for the catch
Had rusted off long since, and there was no latch.

But Thumpy stayed watching, and when he was able
To hear no more voices or sounds from the stable

Came creeping back, for still fresh in his mind
Was the hideous face of the rat left behind

With the baby, and stronger, by far, than his fear
Of the man and his stick, was his love for the dear

Child at the mercy of that savage beast
Who would have been spreading the news of a feast!

He pushed back the door with his front paws and nose
And slipped in, regretting each click of his toes.

Sure enough, his worst fears were about to come true,
For the chief and the rest of that bloodthirsty crew,

Were crouched on the trough in a shadowy ring,
Peering hungrily down, getting ready to spring.

Then rage woke in Thumpy. He would have fought bears
Rearing at bay at the mouths of their lairs.

It could have been lions! He wouldn't have cared.
He'd have taken on elephants, if they had dared

To threaten his prince! Without making a sound
He leapt from the door, and with one further bound

Reached the manger and caught one foul beast in midair
As it sprang for the child. A short squeal of despair

And a snap could be heard, then a thud broke the hush
As the rat hit the floor and lay still. With a rush

Thumpy turned on the others, his blue eyes ice-cold.
But these were no story-tale mice—lean and bold

They were heartless and deadly, and quite a few cats
Had not lived to boast how they'd challenged those rats.

Thumpy lunged for the nearest, but flicking its head
It avoided his teeth and attacked him instead,

Sideswiping his muzzle. He started to yelp,
But stopped just in time, knowing no one could help

If the man should wake up now and chase him away—
So, tasting his blood, he turned back to the fray.

The battle was ugly and fierce, but no sound
Escaped from our hero as, bristling, the hound

Again and again charged and hit or got slashed
Until he was half-blind, his head was so gashed.

But when the old chief fell, the rest of the pack
Turned tail and scuttled off, squeezed through a crack

And vanished! Then Thumpy, legs shaking, ears torn,
Turned back to the manger in which the newborn

Was sleeping in peace still, untouched by a claw.
He sighed, flopped down, pillowed his chin on a paw

Very gently and, blinking the blood from one eye,
Lay beside Jesus till light took the sky.

When Joseph awoke, it was already light.
He lay there awhile, taking in the strange sight

Of rafters and doves' nests, and couldn't think where
He was for a moment, and then, in thin air

Pictured the baby, the shepherds, the kings
The innkeeper's scowl, and, among other things,

The dog that had threatened the child in the night.
He got up, went over, and to his delight,

Found Jesus still sleeping, a smile on his face—
Then noticed, with sudden sharp horror, the place

Where the very same hound was curled up by the manger
Staring at him with one eye that flashed danger.

He stepped back and hurriedly took up his stick,
Advancing on Thumpy, who uttered a thick

Growl and half rose, this time not to escape!
The man was about to lash out, when some shape

Caught the edge of his eye: the slumped form of a rat
As big as he'd ever seen—like a small cat!

Then he noticed another nearby, sprawled and still,
Another! And then, with a spine-tingling chill,

The battle began to take shape in his mind
And he looked at the dog and saw he was half-blind

From a cut near one eye, and his muzzle all caked
With dried blood—and suddenly Joseph's heart ached

For the half-starving creature he'd driven away
Who'd come back, a savior—but all he could say

Was "Good dog!" as he, with a half-sobbing laugh
Of relief and thanksgiving, laid down his staff.

"Good dog!" he repeated. "Stay there, and I'll see
About breakfast for you." Going down on one knee,

He searched through the packets and bundles piled high,
That the shepherds had left, till he found a meat pie,

Then turned back toward Thumpy. The dog growled and stood,
Not trusting the man, though the pie did smell good.

He cocked his head, first to one side, then the other,
Both nostrils a-twitch, each outdoing its brother,

But when Joseph got too close, all of the years
Of beatings and kickings brought back Thumpy's fears

And he bared his teeth, snarling. Then Mary, who'd seen
In a flash how the rats had been killed, stepped between

The two, saying, "Let me try, Joseph. He's scared."
She took the meat pie and, as far as she dared,

Approached Thumpy, making those soft, coaxing coos
That one who loves dogs knows and dogs can't confuse;

And something in Mary's voice, gentle and kind
Calmed Thumpy's fears, and he wagged his behind,

Sat back on his haunches, and thumped his thin tail
On the stable floor, while May picked up a pail

Still half-filled with water, put it and the pie
A few feet from Thumpy, and sat down close by

Very gingerly—still, from the evening before,
No matter how full of grace, painfully sore.

The dog rose and took a step forward, suspicious,
Unused to such treatment. The pie smelled delicious!

Like something right out of his dreams! So he came
Another step, while Mary crooned some sweet name.

He reached the pie, sniffed, gave a tentative lick
Then wolfed down the whole thing. (That he wasn't sick

On the spot was a miracle! Although I think
He'd have downed half a dozen more!) After a drink,

He looked up and saw Mary's beckoning hand,
And, trembling all over, obeyed her command.

Through a hush so profound you could hear the flies hum,
Thumpy came, sniffed her fingers, and licked Mary's thumb.

Then all of his hard-learned defenses caved in
In a moment of trust, and the dog placed his chin

On the kind woman's knee and, with whimpers and cries,
Gazed up into Mary's soft, tear-misted eyes.

Spouting streams of sweet nonsense (which he understood)
She stroked him and scratched him, till it felt so good

Our hero rolled over, exposing his belly
Which got a good scratch too, although it was smelly

Until, brimming over, the dog scrambled up
And dashed round the stable, as wild as a pup

With such yippings and yappings, woofs, growls, snarls, and yelps
You would have believed a whole litter of whelps

Were brawling. But when Jesus started to wail,
Thumpy stopped, bounded over (upsetting the pail)

And, panting, stood still, grinning down at the boy
Till the Prince of Peace calmed down and gurgled with joy.

Well now, there isn't much left to unfold
Of my story. They all knew, without being told,

That Thumpy was theirs now, and that they were his.
When the innkeeper came out to take care of biz

And learned what had happened, the rascal pretended
That Thumpy was his precious hound who'd defended

Many a child, and himself, from great danger,
Until the dog, sniffing that too-well-known stranger,

Snarled, took one fat, sweaty wrist in his jaws,
And would have reached bone—but a word make him pause

From Joseph, who, frowning, took one piece of gold
From those the kings left them—and Thumpy was sold.

They stayed on a few days, while Mary recovered,
And Thumpy, bathed, brushed, and in bandages, hovered

Like Jesus's shadow, still sniffing about
For the rats, who showed whiskers, but never came out.

And then they packed up and set off, after giving
Their tax money, to where the couple was living:

The city of Nazareth, where a soft crib
Lay waiting, along with a rose-bordered bib.

And Jesus grew into a wise, gentle boy
Who never threw tantrums or broke a friend's toy.

"But, Daddy, do you really mean Jesus never
Teased, or got punished, or screamed, ever, ever?"

Well, since you put it like that, I'm not sure
That even a son of God could be that pure.

At times, I suppose, even Jesus, like any
Young boy, may have taken a dime or a penny,

Refused to eat spinach, punched someone at school,
Thrown acorns at squirrels, or broken a rule,

For he, on one side at least, was human too
And must have had bad moments, like me and you.

But wherever he went, Thumpy trotted along
Looking after his prince, filling out, sleek and strong

With good food and care, till, right up to his eyes,
He looked like his forebear who'd won every prize.

He thumped somewhat less, though he still had his fleas
And liked a good scratch, for its sweet, painful ease,

And fought no more rats, though he gave quite a scare
To a cat, now and then, that he chased to its lair,

But mostly was gentle as Jesus, and barked
Very rarely, and all those who saw them remarked

That the growing boy's eyes had the same dreamy look
As his close canine friend's as they sat by a brook

Gazing into the water, or walked by the sea
Looking out to the fishing boats of Galilee

Or beheld, on the streets, as they strolled, munching cheese,
The rich on their horses, the poor on their knees.

And how much his dog's love seeped into the boy
As he grew into that saintly man who took joy

In giving to others, and pardoned the wrongs
That he had to suffer (though all that belongs

To a different story) I really can't say,
But I'm sure that we all, each in his or her way,

Have something to learn from the head on our knee
That looks up at us with such rapt ecstasy

As if each of us was a princess or prince
(Unless a sharp word or a slap, makes it wince—

And even then comes back soon, ready to play
As if nothing'd happened, or we'd been away);

For I know that inside us, as well as the dark
Feelings we all sometimes feel, lies a spark,

(Though sometimes it dwindles to the faintest trace)
Of something that some have called God and some grace—

Though I wouldn't dull its soft glow with a name—
Some spark, that in Jesus was more like a flame,

Which often gets buried by greed, fear, or rage,
As we see every day on the paper's front page,

But that still lies smoldering, somehow survives,
Waiting to help us to live better lives

And shines forth in moments of loving and laughter,
At Christmas especially, but on the days after

As well, here and there, in a smile or a sigh,
The touch of a hand or a dream-cloudy eye…

As yours must be too by now—but my tale's through,
So sweet dreams, and may they, like Thumpy's, come true.